The Valentine Cat

THE
Valentine Cat

by CLYDE ROBERT BULLA

ILLUSTRATED BY LEONARD WEISGARD

TROLL MEDALLION

Published by Troll Associates, Inc.

Printed in the United States of America.

10   9   8   7   6   5   4   3   2   1

Library of Congress Cataloging-in-Publication Data
Bulla, Clyde Robert.
The Valentine cat / by Clyde Robert Bulla; illustrated by Leonard Weisgard.
        p.   cm.
    ISBN 0-8167-3702-9 (lib.)   ISBN 0-8167-3599-9 (pbk.)
    [1. Cats—Fiction.]   I. Weisgard, Leonard, (date), ill.   II. Title.
    PZ7.B912Val   1994   [E]—dc20   94-18353

An Artist's New Beginning

Tell was happier than he had been for a long time. It was good to come home in the evening and find the little cat there. He could talk to the cat. They could even play together.

One night, Tell opened his old paint box. He had some paints left. He had brushes. But he had no canvas.

"No matter," he said.

And he began to paint on the wall.

The longer he painted, the more excited he grew.

"Look!" he said, as he threw down his brush. "There is your picture, big as life. I had forgotten how good it is to paint. Little cat, I've made up my mind to something. If I can't be an artist to please the world, I'll be an artist to please myself."

The Valentine Cat

I

LONG AGO, in a faraway land, a kitten was born in a wood-cutter's barn. He was black all over, except for a snip of white on his forehead. His fur was short and rough. He had pointed ears and a funny, pointed face.

The woodcutter's daughter laughed aloud when she first saw him. The next moment she was sad.

"Poor thing," she said. "What's to become of you?"

Every day she came to see him. She talked to him and held him in her lap. Sometimes he sang. Sometimes he played by leaping at her hand and biting it very gently.

She tried to keep him hidden, but as he grew, he began to play outside the barn. The woodcutter saw him. This was what the girl had feared.

"You know the rule," her father said. "No kittens here."

"Not even one little kitten?" asked the girl.

"We have the mother cat," her father said, "and she is enough."

The girl began to cry.

Her father said no more. He waited until she was asleep that night. Then he carried the kitten away.

He crossed the river in his little boat. He went deep into the woods. He put the kitten down and left him.

The woods were dark and strange. Night birds were calling to one another. The wind made whispering sounds in the trees. The kitten was afraid. He cried in a tiny voice, but there was no one to hear him.

All the next day he looked for food and another home. He stopped at the houses on the edge of the woods. At one house a woman shook her broom at him and children threw sticks. At other houses dogs barked and drove him away.

At last he went back into the woods, and there he stayed.

He learned to eat grasshoppers. They tasted like dry sticks, but they kept him alive. Now and then he was quick enough to catch a wood mouse. In pools along the river he found eels and shellfish.

He grew from a kitten to a cat. Life was not easy for him. He never had enough to eat, and so he was always smaller than most cats. He had no friends. He had no home.

Winter came, with cold days and colder nights. It was harder than ever for him to find anything to eat. It was hard for him to keep warm.

Late one night he stopped at a farm near the woods. In the barnyard was a cart piled high with straw. He climbed into the cart. He made a warm, deep bed in the straw.

In the morning the farmer hitched his horse to the cart and drove away.

The cat liked his bed too much to jump out. Soon he found that he also liked to ride. The cart moved from side to side, and the rocking put him to sleep again.

The farmer drove into the city. There in the market place he sold his load of straw. He tossed it out of the cart.

"A cat! A cat in the straw!" people cried. They shouted and laughed as they tried to catch him.

The cat made a flying leap across the market place. He ran up a pole and onto a roof. He ran away over the rooftops.

Wherever he went, there was more and more of the city. It was as strange to him as the woods had once been.

He ran from everyone he saw. He ran from the horses and carriages. When he was too tired to go any farther, he hid in an alley. He lay there, shaking from fright and cold.

II

IN THE CITY lived a young man named Tell. He had come there with hopes of being an artist, but no one would buy the pictures he painted. He had given up his hopes and gone to work for a shoemaker. All day he nailed the heels on boots and shoes.

Every day was the same. Every night he walked home with his head down and a weary look on his face. People who saw him said to themselves, What a sad young man!

One cold evening he took a short cut home. By a wall in an alley he saw something move. He stopped to see what it was. It was the black cat.

"Ho, little cat!" said Tell. "This is no place for you. You should be sitting by your fire."

The cat was almost frozen. He could not run away.

"Maybe you've no fire to go to," said Tell. "Is that it? Come, I'll take you with me."

He put the cat under his coat and carried him home.

Tell lived at the top of an old tumble-down house. His room was bare and cold.

He lit a candle. He made a small fire in the grate.

When the cat was warm he jumped off Tell's knee and ran under the bed. In the morning he was still hiding there.

Tell left him some bread to eat. That night he brought home milk and a piece of fish. He warmed a bowl of milk and set it on the floor. He put the fish down beside it.

The cat looked out from under the bed.

"Ho, little cat, you've washed your face!" said Tell. There's something white on your forehead. . . . It's a *heart,* little cat. Did you know that?"

At the sound of Tell's voice, the cat hid again.

Tell said nothing more that night. He put out the light and went to bed. In the morning all the milk was gone. So was all the fish, except for one small bone.

The next night, when Tell talked to him, the cat did not hide. After he had been fed, he rubbed against the chair and the table.

"Ah, you're a strange one," said Tell. "What made you so wild, and where did you come from, I'd like to know? But no matter. You have a home now, and I have a cat!"

Tell was happier than he had been for a long time. It was good to come home in the evening and find the little cat there. He could talk to the cat. They could even play together.

Tell brought home a catnip ball. The little cat rolled it about the room. He threw it into the air and caught it in his paws.

At work, Tell thought of the cat playing with the ball.

The shoemaker came by.

"What is the joke?" he asked.

"Joke?" said Tell.

"You were smiling," said the shoemaker.

"Oh," said Tell. "I was thinking of my cat."

"What did he do?" asked the shoemaker.

"He was playing. He is a funny little cat with a heart in the middle of his forehead. Here—I'll show you how he looked." Tell took some brown paper and a piece of charcoal. Quickly he drew a picture. It was a picture of the cat jumping into the air after the catnip ball.

The shoemaker laughed. He took the picture and put it on the wall.

That night Tell said to the cat, "What do you think? Today I drew your picture. Not a bad one, either, and I wasn't half trying."

The cat was lying on the floor with the catnip ball between his paws.

"If I really tried," said Tell, "I might draw a good picture. I might draw a very good picture, indeed."

He found some paper. He took a piece of charcoal from the fire. He began to draw the cat. When he had finished, he was disappointed.

"It isn't bad," he said, "but I need color for your eyes. I need color for the way the light shines on your fur. It would be great fun to *paint* your picture, little cat."

He opened his old paint box. He had some paints left. He had brushes. But he had no canvas.

"No matter," he said.

And he began to paint on the wall.

The longer he painted, the more exited he grew.

"Look!" he said, as he threw down his brush. "I haven't forgotten how to paint. I still remember, little cat. There is your picture, big as life. How do you like it?"

In the morning he looked at the picture again.

"I can do better than that," he said. "I'm sure I can do better."

He ran all the way home that evening. He could hardly wait to paint another picture of the cat.

The next picture *was* better.

He looked at the two cats on the wall.

"I had forgotten how good it is to paint," he said. "Little cat, I've made up my mind to something. If I can't be an artist to please the world, I'll be an artist to please myself."

III

BY THE END of winter Tell had painted one wall of his room. By the end of spring he had painted another.

From floor to ceiling were black cats, little and big. Some were running. Some were climbing. Some were curled up asleep. Behind them were woods and fields and houses. In one corner Tell had painted a cherry tree with a black cat looking out of the branches.

"See, little cat?" he said. "It's going to be one big picture over all four walls."

On summer evenings he liked to go walking. Wherever he went, he saw something new to put into his picture.

Always the cat was with him, riding on his shoulder or walking beside him.

They went to the market place. They walked in the parks. They looked through the iron fence at the royal palace.

Tell said to the cat, "This is the home of our king and queen and the young Princess Florinda. Some day we may see them out on the steps."

But they never saw the royal family on the palace steps. They never saw anyone there except the tall guards in bright red coats.

Sometimes on their walks they met a strange little man. He was thin as an eel. He wore a wide hat that drooped over his face. His clothes were never clean, and his hands were black with soot. He was Ketch, the chimney sweep. He lived across the street from Tell.

Whenever he saw Tell and the cat go by, he looked carefully at the cat. Just the right size, he would say to himself. Just—the—right—size.

Now and then the cat stayed out all day. He never went far. He was always near the house when Tell came home from work.

On an evening in the fall, Ketch saw the cat across the street. Ah, there he is, he said to himself, and all alone, too.

He fished a bit of meat out of the stewpot. He put on his hat and went outside.

He looked up and down the street. There was no one in sight.

"Come, kitty. Come, you pretty little thing," he said in a voice as soft as cream. "See what I've brought you."

The cat sniffed the bit of meat Ketch held out to him. He moved toward it.

Then a coldness touched him just behind the ears. It was the feel of danger.

He drew back, but he was too late. Ketch had made a quick sweep with his hat. The cat was caught beneath it.

Tell came home from work. He looked in front of the house. He looked on the stairs.

He went down the street, asking everyone he met, "Have you seen my little black cat?"

He asked at the chimney sweep's house.

"You've lost your cat? Oh, what a pity!" said Ketch in a voice as smooth as oil. "If I see him, I'll surely let you know."

Days went by. Tell searched the city for the little cat. He could not paint. He could hardly keep his mind on his work. He lay awake at night, hoping to hear a scratch at the door. When he looked at the black cats on the wall, he thought he had never been so lonely before.

IV

AS LONG AS he could remember, Ketch had been a chimney sweep. He climbed up and down chimneys, sweeping out the soot with a broom.

When a chimney was so small he could not get inside it, he cleaned it as best he could with a brush on the end of a pole.

It was hard work. He had often wished for a helper. Now he had one. His helper was the black cat.

He put the cat into a harness. He let him down the small chimneys on a long piece of cord.

Each time the cat fought to get free. He was afraid of the darkness and the wind rushing up the chimney. He tried to catch himself to keep from falling. The more he fought and spread his claws, the better he cleaned the chimney.

He swept out the small chimneys so neatly that Ketch tried him in larger ones. The cat worked very well in crooks and corners.

Ketch was proud of his idea, and he kept it to himself.

Why should I tell the other chimney sweeps? he thought. Let them think of their own ideas.

People said to him, "How do you clean a chimney without going inside it or using a brush on a pole?"

He answered, "I have a magic broom."

They only saw him take something out of a leather bag and pop it down the chimney. Then they saw him draw something up and pop it into the bag. There was no way for them to tell what Ketch's magic broom really was.

All day the cat was either down a chimney or in the leather bag. All night he was locked in Ketch's house.

Sometimes he cried at night.

One evening Ketch heard someone outside his house. He peeped out and saw Tell standing there.

"Good evening, neighbor," said Tell. "I was on my way home, when I thought I heard a cat. It sounded like my own little cat, and I stopped to listen."

"I heard nothing—nothing at all," said Ketch. He closed the door. He caught the cat and threw him down the cellar steps.

"There, Master Chimneysweep, do your crying where no one can hear you," he said, "although what you have to cry about is more than I can see. Don't I feed you every day? Don't I give you a home under my roof? How many other cats have as much?"

Ketch had begun to feel important and proud. All about the city he was known as the man with the magic broom. So many people spoke of him that his name reached the royal palace.

Valentine's Day was coming, and young Princess Florinda asked her father, "Will there be a parade?"

"Yes, my dear, if you wish it," said the king. "Shall I call out the army to march through the city?"

"Please, not the army," said the princess. "I want a *happy* parade, with drums and horns and fiddles playing. I want children to march. I want coaches with red hearts on them."

She asked her mother, "Will there be a Valentine party in the palace?"

"Yes, my dear, if you wish it," said the queen. "Shall I have the ballroom made ready?"

"Please, not the ballroom," said the princess. "It's so big and cold. I want only a small party, and I'd like it in the red room."

The red room was far back in the palace, and it was hardly ever used.

"Why do you want the party there?" asked the queen.

"Because red is the color for a Valentine party," said the princess.

She went running away to have the room made ready. In a little while she was back.

"The fire won't burn in the fireplace," she said. "The smoke comes out into the room."

"There may be birds' nests in the chimney," said the queen.

"We must call a chimney sweep," said the king.

The queen said, "I have heard of one with a magic broom."

"I, too, have heard of this man," said the king. "I shall send for him."

So it happened that when Ketch came home from work that night there was a letter under his door. It was written on thick white paper. At the bottom was the king's seal.

Ketch turned pale when he saw the blue seal. He read the letter twice. He gave a great shout.

"Master Chimneysweep!" he cried to the black cat. "I've been called to the royal palace. The king himself has called for me and my magic broom. I shall be famous. I shall be rich!"

And he danced all about the room.

He was up early in the morning. He dressed in his cleanest clothes. He put the cat into the leather bag and set out for the palace.

A guard let him through the gate. A servant took him up a long stairway.

Oh, proud and happy day! thought Ketch. Here I am in the royal palace. If I clean this chimney well, I may be the next royal chimney sweep.

The servant opened a door that led to the roof. He pointed out the chimney to be cleaned.

Ketch walked across the roof. It was steep, and there was snow underfoot.

Servants watched from the doorway.

Ketch called to them, "Don't come any closer, or the magic may do you harm."

He held his hat over the leather bag. He took out the cat and popped him into the chimney. He let him down on the long cord.

Something moved on top of the palace tower. It was only a crow that had a nest there. But Ketch thought the king himself must be watching from the tower.

He bowed low. In his excitement, he dropped his hat. He tried to catch it, and his feet slipped in the snow. He let go of the cord.

"Help, help!" he cried, as he slid down the roof and over the edge.

V

WHEN KETCH let go of the cord, the cat fell down the chimney. He landed in the fireplace in a cloud of soot and ashes.

Servants came running. One of the maids stood on a table and called for help.

The cat ran under a chair. There was a great bumping and thumping about him. The fur stood up on his back, and the danger spot was cold behind his ears.

Then the room grew quiet.

Princess Florinda was there.

"What *is* the matter?" she asked.

"Oh, Your Highness, something just came down the chimney!" said one of the servants.

"It's something frightful," said another. "It ran under the chair. See? It has a tail so long that there's no end to it."

"It looks like a piece of cord to me," said the princess.

She bent down and looked under the chair.

"So *this* is the chimney sweep's magic broom!" she said.

She pulled gently on the cord. The cat came out from under the chair.

"It's only a cat!" said the servants.

The maid climbed down off the table. "Don't touch him, Your Highness. You'll have soot all over your pretty hands."

"Take him away then," said the princess. "Take this ugly harness off him. Brush him clean and bring him back to me quickly."

She went to her father.

"Where is the chimney sweep?" she asked.

"He lost his magic broom and fell off the roof into a snow-drift," said the king.

"Magic broom, indeed!" said the princess. "It was a cat—a poor little cat that he let down the chimney."

"Bless me!" said the king. "Are you sure?"

"Of course I am," said the princess. "Where is that chimney sweep?"

"In the kitchen, taking hot tea," said the king.

"He must be punished," said the princess.

"Yes, he must be," said the king. "How shall we punish him?"

"Ride him out of the city on a broomstick," said the princess, "and tell him he must never come back."

"Very well," said the king, and it was done.

Two guards seized Ketch and carried him out on a broom-stick.

The servants brought the cat back to the princess. He had been brushed until his fur shone.

"Oh!" she cried. "There on his forehead—a heart!"

She took the cat to the king and queen.

One of the ladies of the court threw up her hands. "What a *common* cat!" she said.

"Common, indeed," said the princess. "Do you know of another cat in the world with a heart in the middle of its forehead? This is a Valentine cat, and he has come to me just in time for Valentine's Day." She asked her father, "Please, may I keep him for my own?"

The queen whispered to the king, "As long as it makes her happy, why not let her keep him?"

"I was going to," the king whispered back. He told the princess, "Yes, you may keep your Valentine cat."

"Oh, thank you—thank you!" said the princess, and she took a ribbon off her dress to make a bow for the black cat's neck.

VI

ON VALENTINE'S DAY the sun was bright, and most of the snow was gone.

"It's such a beautiful day," said Princess Florinda, "I'm going to ride in the parade."

The royal coach was hung with lace and red satin hearts. Six white horses pulled the coach. Ten palace guards marched beside it. Inside sat the princess with the Valentine cat in her arms.

The royal coach led the parade. Then came drummers and fiddlers and horn players. Behind them marched hundreds of children dressed in their best.

People stood along the streets. They called out, "Long live our Princess Florinda!"

The princess waved. Now and then she held up the Valentine cat and waved his paw at the crowds.

All at once the cat stood up. The parade had come to a part of the city he knew.

He knew the street. He knew the houses. He had come home.

In one leap he was out of the coach.

"Come back!" called the princess.

But the cat had already disappeared in the crowd.

"Stop the parade!" cried the princess. "The Valentine cat has run away."

The crowd took up the cry: "The Valentine cat has run away!"

The palace guards told the princess, "Never mind, Your Highness. We'll search until we find him."

Tell had worked all morning.

In the afternoon the shoemaker said, "No more work today. There is a half holiday for the Valentine parade."

Tell watched the parade. He saw the princess's hand as she waved from the royal coach. He shouted, "Long live our Princess Florinda."

Then he went home.

Outside the house he saw a cat.

He thought, How much it looks like my little cat.

The cat began to rub back and forth against the doorstep.

Tell cried out, "It *is* my little cat! It is—it is!"

He picked the cat up. He carried him upstairs.

"Where have you been?" he asked. "How I wish you could tell me!"

The cat sniffed the bed and the chairs and the table. He looked up at Tell and purred.

"Are you glad to be home?" asked Tell. "Oh, but I'm glad to have you. Now I won't be alone. We'll go walking in the old places. And I'll paint again. I'll paint new pictures of you on this wall!"

All the time the palace guards were searching the city. Princess Florinda walked with one of the guards. She called the Valentine cat as she went.

"He knows my voice," she said. "If he hears it, he may come to me."

A boy spoke to her. "Pardon, Your Highness, but are you looking for a little black cat?"

"Oh, yes!" said the princess.

"I saw a man carry such a cat into the old house there," said the boy.

The guard was off. The princess was behind him. They ran into the house. They looked from room to room. They came to the room at the top.

"Open, in the king's name!" shouted the guard.

Tell opened the door.

The guard looked into the room. "There is the cat!" he cried. "Oh, you'll pay for this!"

"Pay for what?" asked Tell. "What have I done?"

"You know very well," said the guard. "You have stolen the princess's cat."

"This cat is mine," said Tell.

"You dare to say the Valentine cat is yours?" said the guard.

Tell began to tremble.

"I have done no wrong," he said.

Princess Florinda ran past the guard into the room.

"There you are!" She held out her arms to the cat. "Why did you run away? I was afraid I would never find you—"

She stopped. She was looking at the painting on the walls. The sun shone down through the skylight. It touched the colors so that they seemed almost alive.

"What a beautiful room!" she whispered.

Tell had fallen on his knees before her.

She asked him, "Who are you?"

"My name is Tell, Your Highness," he said.

"What is your work?" she asked.

"I am only a shoemaker's helper," he said.

"Then who painted all these wonderful things?" she asked.

"I painted what you see here," he said.

The guard spoke. "Your Highness, this man has stolen the Valentine cat. I must take him away."

"I have stolen nothing, Your Highness," said Tell. "If I had known this cat was yours, I should have brought him to you. Once he was mine. Just now I found him outside the house. Cats do come back, you know."

"I don't believe him," said the guard.

"I believe him," said the princess. "It's plain to see the cat once lived here. There are pictures of him all over the walls." She said again, "What a beautiful room!" She asked, "Could you paint my room like this?"

"Your room?" said Tell in surprise.

"My room in the palace," said the princess.

"I could try, Your Highness," said Tell. "I should like nothing better than to try."

"And there are many other rooms in the palace that need pictures," she said. "Come, I'll show them to you."

Tell and the princess and the cat rode away in the royal

coach. Tell met the king and queen. Afterward he sat beside the princess at the Valentine party.

He was given rooms in the palace, and the rooms became his home. Day after day, year after year, he painted, while the princess watched and the cat played about their feet.

The palace stands today, with the paintings still on the walls. There are houses and fields and rivers and trees, all in soft, clear colors that are only a little faded. And on every wall, if you know where to look, you can find the face of the Valentine cat.

ABOUT THE AUTHOR

CLYDE ROBERT BULLA was born near King City, Missouri. He grew up on a farm and attended a one-room schoolhouse where he wrote his first stories and composed his first songs. It was in Missouri that he wrote his first book and worked on a newspaper, doubling as a linotype operator and conductor of a column.

Then Mr. Bulla began to travel. He saw a lot of the United States, Canada, Mexico, and Central America. Later his travels took him to many other countries all over the world. When he saw Los Angeles, he decided to live there. He lives there now, devoting most of his time to writing stories for children. He still travels when he gets a chance.

Mr. Bulla is the author of more than seventy books for young readers. Their backgrounds are as varied as his own interests.

ABOUT THE ARTIST

LEONARD WEISGARD has had a long and distinguished career as an artist, comprising everything from set design and costumes for the ballet to cover paintings for *The New Yorker* magazine. Yet he is perhaps best known for his extraordinary contributions to the field of children's book illustration, and has been honored with the Caldecott Medal. He lives in Denmark.